Repeating

Jean Bell

contents

Prologue

ISABELLA'S POV:

Walking down the main street in town I noticed a crowd of people around a shop window. I pushed through the crowd to get a better look to see the televisions in the window were on the news channel.

"Breaking news: The Government have now declared a 'cleaning' of the city. All people either below the poverty line or lower middle class and further down will now be cleared out and put in other 'safe houses' to provide more space for the overpopulated city we now live in. There is no information about these so-called 'safe houses' as of yet but there have been plans for the demolishment of the areas that these people live in so that the Government can start rebuilding the city faster. It has been said in the press conference that Government officials will be going around with a list of names and taking these people to the 'safe houses' from today for the next few weeks. In other news..."

Shock took over my body as I seemed to automatically make my way back through the crown and towards my falling apart house. I thought I would have had enough money by now to classify myself as average middle class when I moved out here.

With my abusive past I thought this town would be a good change for me but I thought wrong. Im still barely making enough money to put food on the table for myself or pay the bills for this broken down shack of a house. There is no doubt in my mind that im on that list and it terrifies me to no end.

What will the safe houses be like? Are there even any safe houses or were they lying to prevent riots? Are they going to ship us away or kill us?

But anyway, as crappy as my house may be its still mine. I bought it with my hard earned money and I don't want to leave it. Ever.

After arriving home I made myself a cup of tea and sat down on my bed - if you could even call a dirty old mattress on the floor a bed - and that is where I have sat, contemplating what will happen to me for hours until I heard a knock on the door that gave me chills. I know who is on the other side of that door.

I stood up slowly and cautiously walked towards the door, obviously stalling the inevitable. With a shaky hand I twisted the doorknob and cracked the door open, just enough for me to be able to see the two tall muscular men in expensive dark suits and sunglasses. One of the men removed his pair of glasses when he saw me in an effort to seem friendly.

"Good afternoon, are you Isabella Lillian Hill?" the one without glasses asked.

"U-um...Y-yes I am. Who might you be?" I asked, silently praying they weren't here to take me away.

"Oh, well Miss, we just wanted to inspect your home. You know, check for any mold or diseases in the soil and water. Is that alright?"

"Oh, yes that's um that's fine but I have been living here for quite some time now and haven't gotten sick so I don't um I don't think you really need to check anything"

"Well seeing as you're the last house we are checking for the day and it is mandatory that we do this check we promise to be fast"

"Um...okay sure, come in" I said and opened the door wider so that they could come in.

"Would you men like a cup of tea?"

"That would be lovely Miss, thank you" the one without glasses said and I went to the kitchen while they searched the house.

The one with glasses had yet to say a thing but I didn't mind. I don't particularly like talking with anyone, especially strangers. That's why I think babies are the lucky ones on this earth because not only do they not have to speak - because they can't - but they have no worries or cares.

As I reached up for the glasses on the shelf I heard the footsteps of the men coming closer. Figuring they were just searching in the kitchen I didn't bother to turn around. That was my second mistake. The first mistake was believing their lie and letting them into my house. My third mistake? Well that was being naïve enough to think I could skip town and avoid being taken.

I felt a sudden pain in the back of my head and then everything went black. When I awoke I was strapped to a metal table. The bright light on the ceiling burned my eyes as I had nowhere to look but straight into it.

Trying to move my arms and legs off the metal table only ended with me catching the attention of my captors as the rattling of the chains connecting to the padded straps clanged against the table.

"Well well well, looks like sleeping beauty has finally woken up." a soft feminine voice said from somewhere behind me.

Frightened, I tried to move my head to search for the voice but it began to feel heavy and I could barely hold it up anymore. I wined and tried to move my arms but they began to feel heavy too, my legs soon followed suit.

What is going on? I thought to myself.

My eyelids felt heavy as the want of sleep suddenly appeared as if I had not slept in the last 48 hours. I opened my mouth, wanting to ask what was going on but the same soft voice shushed me and told me to rest as a hand came down to pet my hair in an effort to coax me into sleep.

Slowly, however, it began to work and I foundmyself surrounded by darkness once again. The last feeling I had was a prick in my neck and the soft voice whispering that everything will be alright.

CHAPTER 1

Another test, another negative. What am I going to tell Leo? What if there is something wrong with me and he leaves me? What about the boys? I got their hopes up for nothing!

I sat on Leo's and my shared bed, looking down at yet another batch of pregnancy tests that all say negative. My eyes began to water and the tears soon fell freely as I thought more about the possibility of Leo, my love, leaving me for another because I could not bare us the little girl we both dreamed of having.

Stuck in my thoughts I missed the sound of the front door opening and closing, the sound of my love yelling out that he was home, his footsteps as he made it up the stairs towards me. It was only when he bent down in front of me, lifting my head up with two fingers under my chin, did I finally acknowledge his presence. He tried to wipe away my tears by there just kept falling, never ending.

"What's wrong, mio amore?" he asked softly as a sob racked through my body.

I stayed silent and handed him the tests. His face contorted into one of sadness and understanding before he stood and picked me up off the bed and into his arms.

He silently slipped off his shoes and laid me back down on the bed before laying next to me. His arms circled my waist, my head lay on his chest listening to his heartbeat while he whispered sweet words into my ear.

"Im sorry I can't give us what we wanted and I just want you to know that I have accepted it." I spoke into his chest knowing he could hear me fine.

He pulled my head away and cradled it in his view.

"What do you mean, Tesoro?" His voice was soft as he spoke, his thumb caressing me cheek.

"You are going to leave me for another woman who will be able to give you what you want because I cannot"

"What on earth are you talking about, amore? I love you and only you. Nobody on this earth could ever replace you." He said slowly, making sure I understood every word before he pushed my head to once again lay gently against his chest, one hand brushing through my hair, the other rubbing up and down my back.

After staying in that position for a while Leo rolled us over and switched on the television in our room.

"Breaking news: In the past few days there has been a sudden overflow of children, particularly newborns, in orphanages around the country. Care-takers are pleading to the public to come and adopt the children as by the day there is less and less room in these facilities. At the moment there are cases of up to 4 newborns sharing one crib..."

I gasped in shock at the news story, horrified at the fact that there are these adorable little creatures being squeezed together because of the lack of space while we have more than enough room for one of them. Tears gathered in my eyes and I looked up at Leo who was already looking down at me.

"Would you like me to arrange a meeting at one of those orphanages, Tesoro?" he asked softly as caressed my cheek with his thumb. I could only nod in reply, not trusting my voice after my emotional breakdown earlier. "Then it will be done, amore, it will be done." He whispered and began stroking my head until I eventually fell asleep.

ISABELLA'S POV:

Waking up again I felt different. Everything still felt heavy but I found that if I concentrated hard enough I could wiggle my arms around a little as well as my legs.

I curled up my fingers into a fist on my left hand and brought it up to my eye to rub it but I couldn't lift my arm that high. I whined from my struggle and confusion on where I was and what is wrong with my body.

I managed to move my head a little bit and look around the room I was in. I think I am starting to go insane but I noticed that everything was bigger. Did I shrink?

My whines seem to have alerted someone outside the room because a moment later the sound of a door opening and closing was heard and a young lady was looking down at me from where she stood near my head.

"Hey sweetheart. Did you have a good sleep?" she cooed down at me before bringing her hands towards me and cradling me to her chest.

There was a sudden strong urge to cry, the confusion and struggle becoming all too much. The tears gathered in my eyes and a wail left my lips, frightening me at first when it sounded like a baby's wail, but soon I didn't care. I cried from confusion, I cried from stress and I cried from the knowledge that I will never get to see my home again, everything I worked for gone within a moment.

"No, no shhh. Don't cry sweetie. Its okay...everything is going to be okay" the lady cooed while rocking back and forth in her arms.

My head lay in the crook of her elbow while she rocked me and I would be lying if I said that it wasn't relaxing. Slowly, my cries stopped and my eyes began to droop and finally, darkness.

CHAPTER 2

I awoke in the morning to stray hairs gently being moved behind my ear, followed by a soft trail of kisses starting from the back of my ear, ending with a soft passionate kiss on my lips.

With a sigh of delight I opened my eyes to stare straight into Leo's. He smiled and pecked my lips again before telling me that it was time to wake up. I groaned in reply - which made him chuckle - but got up anyway and went straight to the shower.

After getting ready for the day I went down stairs to cook breakfast for the boys only to be surprised by the sight of Leo in his suit, jacket on the back of his chair at the table while he stood at the stove, dress shirt sleeves rolled up to his elbows, my apron tied around his front and a spatula in his hand as he flipped the pancakes he had been making on the stove.

I walked towards him and wrapped my arms around him from be-hind.

"You don't have to make breakfast for everyone but thank you" I said as he twisted around and brought me to his chest.

"I just thought that you had quite an emotional night last night and you would like to sleep in a little more before being plunged into the hectic morning with the boys" he expressed and then held my head in his hands, tilted my head up and kissed my forehead in a tender, loving way.

I whispered a thank you before reaching up to peck his lips, although I didn't quite make it which made him chuckle and bend down slightly. Then, with one hand on the small of my back, he led me to my seat and sat me down. Not a moment later was the most beautifully set out breakfast placed down in front of me.

With a smile of thanks I took a sip of the coffee he had just placed in my hands. Heaven. That is the only way I can describe this morning, and to think I haven't even left the house yet.

Our peace and quiet didn't last very long as shouts and heavy foot-steps soon came barreling down the staircase and into the kitchen. Once the boys entered the room, one stern look from Leo had them clam and quiet while they made their way to the table.

After everyone had sat down and was beginning to eat, the boys in a rush to get to school, Leo cleared his throat and began to make his announcement.

"Boys, I've decided that you will not be going to school today, there's too much to do."

"What is there to do?"

"Don't you worry about it mio amore, but im going to be driving you to work."

"No its fine, you don't need to, really."

"Not a chance Tesoro, it'll spoil the surprise. Now, boys, ill let you stay here and relax a bit while I drive your madre to work so when I get back I want the three of you ready to go, we are going to be on a tight schedule today."

"Yes sir" all three boys said together.

With a small clap of my hands I began to stand up to clear the table but was stopped by a gentle hand on my wrist.

"No, no don't get up amore I'll clear your plate, you just go and get your purse and coat."

I nodded and said a quick thank you and gave him a kiss on the cheek. As I waked around the table I place a kiss on each of my sons cheeks and we told each other goodbye and I love you. And finally, when I got my coat and purse Leo returned and met me at the garage door.

"Ready to go, bellezza?" Leo asked. {Beauty}

Nodding in return he placed a hand on the small of my back, opened the door and led me to the car, opening the door and sitting me in the passenger seat like the gentlemen he is.

ISABELLA'S POV:

I awoke again to the feeling of being picked up and the urge to cry returned. The urge being too strong to resist I let out a wail, and being confused as to why the cries sounded like a newborns just made me cry harder. Everything has seemed to turn upside-down and I don't know how and I don't know why.

All these questions were running through my head. Where am I? Why is everything suddenly so big? Why cant I move? Why do I feel so small?

I was so consumed by my thoughts that I didn't feel myself being rocked nor did I notice my cries had dulled to small whines. I curled my hands into fists and slowly opened my eyes only to come face to face with a huge breast, clothed obviously, thankfully.

Unfortunately for me though the woman that was holding me sat down on a nearby chair and gently I was moved around so that she could do what I would never have expected in a million years but at the same time answered all my questions.

Slowly, when I was moved out of the way, the woman - who I noticed was middle aged after she had turned me around and held me in one of her hands facing her - unbuttoned her shirt and then unhooked her bra. When her breast tumbled out she brought me closer and im ashamed to say that I didn't work this out sooner.

They had turned me into a newborn. Those injections. That is probably what they are doing to all of the poor people. There are no safe houses. They lied. They stole me from my home, took everything I worked for and made me disappear. How could this happen? This is so wrong!

Actually, speaking of wrong, my little newborn mouth is, as of now, about two inches away from this lady's nipple. She tapped me lightly on the back wanting me to willingly move myself towards the horrid nipple but I refuse.

"Oh come on sweetie pie, you need to eat so that you can be a big strong girl" she cooed down at me in a baby voice.

I hate it. I hate that condescending voice. I hate that I cant move. I hate that im small. I hate that im probably wearing a diaper and I hate that now that I thought of it I've probably used the diaper because I cant control anything I do. I just hate everything about this horrible situation and I just want to cry, and so I did.

The tears gathered in my eyes and before I could stop myself my mouth opened to let out a cry but, to my misfortune, the woman took my open mouth as a chance to shove her nípple in my mouth. I struggled a bit but the woman shushed me.

"Shh just drink sweetie its good I promise, you'll really like it." she cooed in that stupid baby voice again.

Unfortunately, while trying to swallow my own spit so I don't dribble and look even more like a baby, I sucked up some of the breast milk from the nípple that was forced into my mouth. It actually wasn't that bad if im being honest.

"That's it darling, isn't that yummy? Oh you are such a good girl." she cooed and stroked my head and ran a finger gently across my cheek.

One of my hands came up to rest on her breast and curled into a fist in attempt to grasp onto something but there was nothing so my hand just kept curling and uncurling. The more I drank the milk the fuller my stomach get and the heavier my eyelids became and very soon all I saw was darkness.

CHAPTER 3

LEONZIO'S POV:

"I will pick you up in about 4 hours okay?" I told my beautiful wife as we stood outside her café.

"Can you just tell me what the surprise is already?" she pleaded, her brown eyes looking up at me. I could see the excitement for her surprise pooling around. She's going to love this.

"No I cant amore but you need to get to work now. Ill see you later okay?"

"Okay" she sighed which made me smile wide.

After placing a soft kiss to her lips and saying our I love you's I went back to the car and drove home to get the boys.

"Okay Luciano, you are going to take Theo in your mothers car and Max, you're with me. We are going to the shopping center to get supplies and I want it done fast because we still have to build everything. Am I understood?" I ordered them when I stepped back into the house.

"Yes sir." They said together and followed me back to the cars.

Once they were all in the cars I made sure Luce was following me in his mothers car all the way to the shopping center. Max sat in the passenger seat next to me.

"What's the surprise?" he asked as I parked the car in the shopping center parking lot.

"I can't tell you but im sure the three of you will figure it out." I told him and got out of the car to meet the other boys. Once Max was out of the car I locked it and continued to the front doors of the shopping center, my sons following close behind me.

When we got inside I turned to them. "Okay I have a list of things we need to get and we need to do it fast because it takes a long time to build. Now, when we get home I need you to put everything in the room that is closest to your mothers and mine. Understand?" I instructed and they replied with a yes sir and we walked into the first store.

Almost an hour later and we had purchased a light pink bassinet, changing table, crib, playpen, baby bottles, pacifiers, diapers, baby carrier, stroller, car seats, baby bath, blankets, toys, teething rings, baby clothes and baby monitors; the best, most expensive one available. It comes with a camera. I also called some guys to come with extra furniture for he room to decorate it.

When we got home I unlocked the room Gemma and I had painted a few months ago when the boys went on a camping trip. The crib and changing table took a good two hours to build - about an hour for each item - but the bassinet only took a couple of minutes to put together and move to Gemma and my shared room.

As fast as possible the boys put all the things away as I folded the clothes and set up the monitors. I had already called the orphanage last night and the told me about their youngest child who is now a day old. I was able talk them into e-mailing me a photo and some details so I could get the right size clothes and diapers.

After putting everything in their place I went downstairs to see how the boys were doing before confirming my appointment time at the orphanage. I walked into the kitchen and saw that everything was unpacked and in its place, the boys watching TV in the next room.

"Okay boys, I'll be back in a few hours with your mother so behave while im gone" I told them sternly.

"Wait, dad, can I go out for a bit?" Max asked from where he lay on the floor.

"Why? Where are you going?"

"This new Xbox game came out yesterday and I didn't have time to get it and I wanted it go pick it up today before its sold out." he explained.

"Fine but I want you back before I come home or there will be trouble. Okay?"

"Yes sir" he said and jumped up and headed for the door but I grabbed the back of his collar as he ran passed me, knocking him back a few steps.

"First, help me set the baby carrier in the back seat."

"Okay. Can you drop me off on the way?"

I sighed. "Fine, hurry up"

"Yes sir" he said and ran the other way towards my car that still had the carrier in the trunk.

After we locked it in correctly Max hopped into the passenger seat and I closed the back door before hopping into the drivers seat and backing out of the driveway. Quickly dropping Max off I made my way to Gemma.

Walking into Gemma's store is one of my favorite things in this world. The way the smell of her baked goods and coffee hitting my face an relaxing me and then, as I walk further into the store the slight smell of old books mixing into the already mouthwatering smell leaves me completely at peace.

However, what brings the store together is the homey feeling. The warm and comforting essence that the little store gives out is the same as walking into your mothers arms after she has baked a fresh batch of cookies. It's the most amazing feeling in the world.

"Leo!" Gemma squealed as she made her way over to me in her frilly, girly apron with flour, egg and chocolate stains. But what made me grin the widest as she came over to me, the smudges of chocolate on her cheeks, noes and forehead. She is too adorable for her own good.

"Tesoro" I said in a soft voice and gently pecked her lips. "Come, its almost time for you to see your surprise, amore."

"You're still not going to tell me?" she asked, looking up at me with those amazing chocolate brown eyes of hers and I almost gave in and told her.

I shook my head with a chuckle. "Go take off your apron" I said and lifted my hand up to her face, swiping my hand along her chocolate covered cheek, "and don't forget to wipe your face" I ended with a laugh as I brought my chocolate covered thumb to my mouth.

With a giggle she turned around and ran to the kitchen to tell the other workers that she was leaving and then ran out to go change in the staff room. I chuckled at her silliness and began to undo my tie so I could use it as a blindfold so she wouldn't see the baby carrier and connect the dots before I wanted her to.

When she came back I spun her around and tied my tie around her eyes and tightened it - not too much to hurt her or pull her hair at the back - before hooking her arm with mine and led her carefully to the car.

The whole way to the orphanage Gemma kept asking me what the surprise was and where we were going in hopes of me actually giving her more of an answer than a simple 'you'll see' accompanied by a chuckle which always earned me a huff as she crossed her arms over her chest.

It wasn't a long drive, only around 30-45 minutes until we arrived at the orphanage. The smile on my face made my cheeks hurt but I didn't wipe it away, instead, I parked the car in front of a two story building and got out. I walked around to the passenger side of the car to let Gemma out and once again, carefully led her to the front of the house, in view of the wooden sign that said 'Sunshine Orphanage'.

I took her blindfold off and pointed her to face the house. I heard a gasp fall from her lips before she spun around and leaped into my arms, hugging me and squealing. And somehow, my smile got bigger.

CHAPTER 4

LEONZIO'S POV:

"Hello and welcome to Sunshine Orphanage. Can I help you two with anything?" the young lady at the front desk asked us.

"Yes, I have an appointment for 2:15pm." I told her. An excited squeal from beside me and I looked down with a smile at my beautiful wife.

"Leonzio Nicolosi?" she asked to confirm and I confirmed her question with a nod. "Okay I'll just call down Victoria, she just fed the babies."

"Its fine we can just sit here for a bit." I replied with a smile and got my wife to calm down enough to sit still in a seat for more than 5 seconds.

"I cant believe this! I didn't think you were serious about this!" she whisper-yelled in excitement.

"Wait, so does that mean that you don't want to be here?" I asked jokingly which, of course, earned me a slap on the arm.

"I just cant believe this. Just when I thought I couldn't love you any more than I do, you go and do something like this and I can't help but swoon like I did when we were dating." she sighed and shook her head lightly with a smile.

"You haven't seen anything yet, amore, just wait till we get home." I whispered to her in her ear and pecked her cheek.

When I sat up straight again a middle aged woman entered the room, stopped for a moment to speak with the girl at the front desk before making her way over to us. I stood as she neared, Gemma following a second later.

"Good afternoon, you must be Leonzio. Im Victoria and it's a pleasure to meet you." she said with a kind smile and an outstretched hand.

"Nice to meet you too, Victoria. This is my wonderful wife Gemma." I introduced and shook her hand in greeting.

"Its lovely to meet you, Victoria." Gemma said from where she stood next to me, a giant smile on her face.

"Its nice to meet you too, Gemma" Victoria smiled back her and then clapped her hands together. "Okay so would you like to see her now?"

"Oh yes, yes please!" Gemma squealed and bounced on her toes slightly in excitement. Both Victoria and I laughed which made Gemma look down and blush but not lose her grin.

"Well then lets get a move on. She's upstairs." Victoria said and led the way up.

Soon we stopped in front of a window, one that you would see in a hospital's maternity ward, behind the window was a medium sized room filled with clear cots in rows, filling up the room. There were so many newborns in that room, too many to be in an orphanage. Honestly, it was sad to see.

Wordlessly, Victoria opened the door a few steps away from us and picked up the most adorable child I have ever laid my eyes on, the picture I was sent does not do justice to the real thing. She's so small I wouldn't be surprised if she fit comfortably in one of my hands alone. She looks so fragile, I don't think I will have it in me to actually hold her in fear of dropping her.

Victoria came back out with little girl and asked if Gemma wanted to hold her because my eyes were trained on the child and were not leaving anytime soon, my mind was blank of everything at the moment.

Suddenly, two hands clapping appeared in front of my eyes and I snapped back to reality.

"Welcome back Leonzio, would you like to see her file now?" Victoria asked, amusement swirling in her eyes.

"Yes please, Victoria that would be great" I said with a kind smile. Victoria turned around and went to a table with some files that stood next to the door to the newborns room. She rummaged through the pile of documents before she picked up the one she wanted and walked back over and handed it to me.

Opening it I saw a photo of what will soon be my little girl, underneath it was all of her personal and medical information.

'FIRST NAME: ISABELLA

MIDDLE NAME: LILLIAN

LAST NAME: UNKNOWN

MOTHER: LILLIAN

FATHER: UNKNOWN

DATE OF BIRTH: 17/05/2016

HEIGHT: 15in

WEIGHT: 3.5lb

ALLERGIES: NONE

OTHER NOTES: All around healthy child, size and weight may be a concern with food portions but not a problem.

"What happened to her mother?"

"She died during childbirth apparently. I heard she never even got to hold her, very sad."

"Then how did you get her name?"

"Well, I was notified that her mothers name was Lillian but because she came randomly off the street with no previous record we don't have her last name, she refused to give it to the doctors, so I figured it would be nice for her to have at least a little part of her mother. 'Isabella' though, that's because when ever she opens her eyes she seems to look around and judge her surroundings. She seems very smart and it was only by coincidence that her mothers favorite movie to watch was 'Beauty and the Beast' so, of course, she had to be named after 'Belle', the smart princess of the movie."

"That's lovely" I said, honestly touched at how much they cared for this little bundle of joy. Victoria nodded and whispered a quick 'I'll leave you three alone' before walking down the hall and out of sight.

I immediately turned towards Gemma and Isabella who were still standing where Victoria and I had left them. Gemma was holding

Isabella close to her chest protectively as if someone was going to snatch her away at any moment. My smile grew at the sight.

"Did you find out what her name is?" Gemma questioned in a soft voice as to not wake the baby. She didn't take her eyes off her as she spoke to me.

"Yes, her name is Isabella, Isabella Lillian Nicolosi" I answered with a smile as I added in my last name in ownership of the beautiful creature in my wife's arms.

"Beautiful" she whispered out so softly I almost missed it. Tears gathered in her eyes as she continued to look down at her before she snapped her head up to look into my eyes and with a watery whisper she said "She's perfect. Thank you for this Leo." And with that, her attention was back on Isabella.

CHAPTER 5

LEONZIO'S POV:

"Okay so if you would just sign here once more I can go fetch her birth certificate for you and then if you don't have anymore questions you are free to go with your new baby girl." She said pointing to the dotted line the I signed a moment later. "Great! Now im just letting you know as part or protocol I have done a background check on you both and you are in the clear so I wont need to be doing any house visits so don't you worry. Also, as Jessica, the girl at the front desk, probably mentioned earlier, I just fed her a little while ago and put her to sleep so she wont wake up for another couple of hours." Victoria informed me.

"From a bottle?" Gemma asked.

"Oh no silly. Part of the reason me and a few other ladies work here is because we still produce breast milk which enables us to feed the little ones."

"But I can't produce anymore" said Gemma worriedly from next to me.

"Its okay, you'd be surprised by how many women come in here to adopt but don't think about ways of actually feeding the child. We provide doctor prescribed pills that help with the problem. The first one we give free with a prescription but after that you go to the pharmacy and they will top you up." Victoria told us as she handed me a small white paper bag that held the pills and prescription. She would have given the bag to Gemma but she refused to put Aurora down since she was placed in her arms.

"Are there any side effects that I should know about?" Gemma asked.

"Well, the first few days as your breast get bigger and full of milk they will ache quite a bit. Just make sure you remember its two pills a day, one after breakfast and one after dinner so you wont have to worry about not having milk in the early hours of the day." Victoria told us while packing up the files to place in a folder.

Victoria walked to the other side of the room and retrieved a piece of paper and walked back to me. She gently placed it down on the table in front of me next to the stack of adoption papers.

"This is her birth certificate. I'm sure you two have done this before, Isabella's name and all other information is already on it so all you two need to do is sign your names as mother and father and then she is officially yours." Victoria said with a smile.

After we both signed the paper Victoria made a copy before she slipped it into a plastic pocket. She gave made a copy of Isabella's personal information as well and placed everything in a folder with the birth certificate and handed it to me. Then came the last bits of information.

"When she wakes up I urge you to not have a lot of people crowding around her. Within the past day and a half of her being alive she has woken up in many different places and I know she will wake again in another environment so just be careful. She will be confused and scared so don't worry if you cant calm her down when she cries, it took me almost 2 hours." Victoria informed us.

Once we told her we understood and asked if there was anything else Victoria said no and allowed us to leave with Isabella. Getting into the car, Gemma was pleasantly surprised by the baby carrier strapped down behind the drivers seat, a warm blanket already laying across it for Aurora.

The whole drive home Gemma kept glancing back to check on Isabella, as if this whole thing was a dream that would disappear at any moment. She watched her sleeping face through the mirror I clipped on at the end of the carrier. The smile never left her face.

By the time we drove into our street it had started to rain heavily so I parked the car in the garage once we got home. I opened my door and stepped out and then, being the gentleman that I am, I ran over to open Gemma's door and help her step down from the car.

I told her to head inside to the boys while I get Isabella out of her carrier in the backseat. Unfortunately, while I was unbuckling Isabella from her carrier she woke up. Her big brown eyes looked everywhere before landing on me and then her face scrunched up cutely before she let out a wail, moving her arms up and down and slightly kicking her tiny little feet.

Quickly, I lifted her into my arms and gently rested her head on my chest, just under my shoulder and bounced up and down and swayed side to side, softly shushing her to get her to calm down. I slowly made my way inside while calming her down and saw Gemma running to me, the boys trailing behind her.

"What happened?" Gemma asked as she gently smoothed down the tuff of hair that Isabella had on her head.

"I was unbuckling her and she just jerked awake and started crying." I said. By now her wails have turned into adorable little hiccups and sniffles as I continued to bounce slightly up and down.

"Can we see her?" Luciano asked as he stepped forward.

I gave Gemma a look, asking if it was okay to have this many people around. She nodded in reply and I gently placed the tiny child in her arms. I watched as Isabella's big brown eyes looked around at everything and I noticed that when she looked up at Gemma she snuggled deeper into her arms.

Luciano was the first of the boys to come and see Isabella. He didn't say a word as he raised his hand and softly stroked his index finger down her puffed out cheek and then moved down to one of her hands and played with her tiny fingers. Isabella, in return grasped it like her life depended on it. He moved to the side with a smile after placing a soft kiss to her forehead.

Next was Theodore, he smiled bright as Isabella's eyes landed on him. I heard him whisper "She's so tiny" before stroking the little hair she had on her head. Just like his brother before him, he played with her fingers before she grabbed one of his and held on for dear life. He then moved to the side, his smile not once leaving his face after he kissed her chubby cheek.

Last was Max, although he couldn't wipe the smile from his face as he saw the tiny girl and I could tell that he was nervous and cautious around her. It looked as though he thought that she was a glass doll and if he were to touch her or hold her too strong he would break her. However, he smiled a watery smile when she grasped his finger in a tight hold, as if she knew what he was thinking and wanted to prove him wrong. He let out a laugh as he backed away after placing a gentle kiss on her tiny hand.

Gemma smiled up at me with tears in her eyes from the quiet, emotional moment between our sons and our new daughter. I smiled down at her and softly asked her to pass Isabella to one of the boys as the surprise wasn't over yet.

She hesitated for a moment before she reluctantly handed Isabella to Luciano who was so nervous he would drop her he had to sit on the couch to cradle her. Gemma and I laughed lightly at that as I led her out of the room and up the stairs.

I grabbed Gemma's hand and steered her towards Isabella's room for the final part of her surprise and with a gasp she took in the room. She turned to me, tears brimming in her eyes as she ran towards me and pushed her face into my chest. My arms, on reflex, wrapped around her tightly as she mumbled multiple thank you's into my chest. When she pulled away she had tears running down her face.

"From your reaction I take that you like the room" I say with a smile as I wiped the tears from her cheeks, "No need to cry, amore" I whisper and place a gentle kiss on her forehead.

"It perfect Leo, I love it so much. I can't thank you enough!" she exclaimed as she gazed up at me with a watery smile. I smiled back down at her before I captured her lips in a short but passionate kiss.

"I love you Gemma, so much, and I would do anything to keep that smile on your face for as long as I possibly can. I love you" I told her sincerely as I gazed into her eyes, my hands holding her head up to look at me.

"I love you too Leo, and I will never stop, not even for a second" she whispered passionately and I captured her lips in yet another passionate kiss, showing her my love and desperation for her through that one kiss.

When we finally broke apart I suggested we head back downstairs to check on the boys and Isabella. The whole way down, the giant smile on my face never left as I trailed behind Gemma. Upon entering the living room we saw Theo and Max sitting on either side of Luc and as we stepped further into the room I was able to locate a sleeping Isabella in Luc's arms, one of her tiny fists clutching his shirt, the other gripping his index finger for dear life.

After Gemma snapped a photo on her phone she walked over to the boys and gently took Isabella into her arms - ignoring the soft protest coming from the boys mouths - and made her way upstairs to place her in her new crib.

CHAPTER 6

A/N This chapter is the end of the last chapter but in Isabella's POV.

Enjoy :)

ISABELLA'S POV:

When I woke up I noticed I was in a car, even worse was the fact that I was in one of those horrid baby car seats that faces the back. My eyes searched for any possible escape but then I was reminded of my limp arms and legs and knew I wouldn't get far if I even had a chance to escape.

My eyes finally caught the face of a man who was staring into my eyes in awe. He looks - to me - like a giant, his face gentle but I could tell that his angry face could send even the most evil of people running for the hills with one glare. The way he stared, it was as if he was waiting to see what I would do now that I was awake and with these urges that I keep trying to resist I knew, we both knew what was about to happen.

My face scrunched up and tears poured down my cheeks while I wailed loudly. It was so hard to fight these urges. I don't want to act like the baby I appear to be but its beginning to become too difficult and I end up giving in anyway out of exhaustion. This fact, of course, added to the tears that spilled down my cheeks and I couldn't stop it.

The giant picked me up and pulled me to his chest with my head resting just under his shoulder, one of his hands covering my entire back all the way to my knees. Either im really small or he has freakishly large hands, whatever it is I didn't care anymore. The baby side of me overpowered my fighting adult self and I officially had no control over my body, that being shown by the way my cheek rubbed slightly against the giants shirt as his swaying and bouncing began to calm me down.

I faintly heard him shushing me softly, his breath slightly fanning the little hair I know I now have on my head. A moment later I heard the car door close and he began walking to another door nearby as my wails turned into sniffles and hiccups.

The sound of rushing footsteps made me more aware of my surroundings in fear of who it may be but I couldn't freeze up or look around like I would have liked to because of the strong hand holding me tight to the giants chest and my lack of control over my own body. I jerked slightly when I felt a different hand on my head, smaller and much smoother than the giant who's arms im still in.

I was suddenly but carefully pulled from the giants arms and place into much more delicate and thin arms. Looking up I saw a women and the baby side of me snuggled closer to her breast from my laying position in her arms. A strange feeling of content filled me as we stared at each other, her motherly presence calming me slightly before my attention was caught on what had touched my cheek.

I turned my head and was met with three boys, men, man-boys. They were all as gorgeous as each other and I couldn't stop staring at them, taking in as much detail as I can. The one stroking my cheek I guessed is the oldest. His hand moved from my cheek to my hand which automatically grasped his finger in a death lock, not wanting this gorgeous man-boy to leave.

Unfortunately he did move to the side but only for the second man-boy to appear in my line of vision. Just like the other man-boy, his smile was so wide that I thought his face would break, but he has an amazing smile. He gently stroked the little hair that I have on my head before moving to my hand like the other man-boy had done.

Once again, my hand gripped his finger tightly without hesitation or thought.

When he too moved to the side the last man-boy stood in front of me. He looked at me uneasy but with a smile. His eyes told me that he wanted to be cautious, as if I would break with a single touch, so, when he came to play with my tiny hand I grasped his finger with all my might while staring him right in the eye. I am not some glass doll and with a laugh he understood what I was trying to say.

I was too focused on the room I was in to notice that the giant was speaking before I was suddenly moved to first man-boys arms and was jerked lightly as he sat on the couch, obviously afraid he would drop me if he were standing. The other two sat beside me and they were all looking down at me.

"Hey there baby, we're your new big brothers" he said with a smile "im your oldest brother Luciano but you can call me Luc, you know, when you can talk." he let out a nervous chuckle when he said that. Luc carefully lifted the top half of my body up so that I could see the brother on his right.

"Hi there Isabella, im Theodor your second oldest brother" he said and then with a chuckle he added "and when you can talk you can call me Theo."

Luc carefully turned me around so that I was facing the other brother on his left side.

"Hi gorgeous, my name is Max and I may not be the oldest out of us three but I am the coolest." He said making the others snort. Luc, distracted by his brothers let his hand slip down slightly and was now not supporting my head which made it fall back and when I tried to lift it myself it just wobbled uncomfortably.

When he noticed my head flinging around he muttered a few curses under his breath before laying me back down in his arms and pulling my body closer to his chest until my cheek was pressed up against his t-shirt.

The sudden urge to sleep hit me with a strong force and my tiny mouth opened wide as I let out a yawn. My hands curled into fists as I raise them so that I can stretch a bit while my eyes closed but they shot open again as I heard awing from above me.

I felt a Luc's thumb stroke my cheek as I snuggled further into his chest, the baby side of me still in full control of my body. Slowly though, from the warmth of Luc's body and those of Theo and Max that surrounded me, matched with the calming strokes of Luc's thumb against my cheek I began to fall asleep for what is probably the forth time today.

I woke up again in a big crib on my back staring at a white ceiling that both reminded me of that hospital-like room I was in but relaxed me at the same time. Wanting to keep the peace I didn't make a noise until another urge filled my body and my stomach made a sound it had never made before.

It was strange. When I was normal I could go a few days with little to no food and my stomach would never make that noise and to be honest it scared the crap out of me which just made the urge to cry grow until a loud mix between a wail and a scream left my lips and once it started I couldn't stop it.

I heard rushed heavy footsteps outside my door before it burst open to reveal the giant. He quickly walked over to the crib and looked down at me, concern clouding in his eyes as he lifted me to his chest.

"Shh little one, daddy's here. Its okay, everything is okay shhh" he said in a soft voice as he swayed back a forth but it didn't help my crying. It wasn't until my stomach made another dying whale noise did he actually know what was wrong.

"Ahh so you're a hungry little one aren't you? Well, lets get you changed first and then we'll go down and see if mummy is able to feed you yet." He said before making his way to a table that I wasn't able to see from inside the crib.

Wait! Did he just say change? Change what?

And that's when I felt it. As if everything I have been through so far wasn't embarrassing enough then I have officially hit rock bottom. Because of my body's lack of inner strength I have managed, while sleeping, to both wet and mess the diaper I was put into.

I was so embarrassed and uncomfortable that not only did I cry throughout the whole change but also after it when we left the room and began to make our way downstairs. No amount of comfort from the giant who calls himself 'daddy' could calm me down until I was placed in the woman's arms. It was something about her motherly aura that just calmed me and maybe it was just because the only comfort I got from my own, real mother was when she threw an icepack at me to help heal my bruises that she and my father caused so that nobody would suspect anything.

Come to think of it, I've only been here with these strange people for less than a day and so far I have gained three kind - from what I've seen so far - older brothers, a 'mother' who holds me as if she were holding the world in her arms and a 'father' who looks at me with such overwhelming love, adoration and care and makes me feel like the safest person in the world when he holds me close. They have kept me warm and happy and accepted me into their family without a second thought.

From what I gather from the giant, I will be getting food soon, something I used to have to work and beg for and even then it would only be a small portion of my parents leftovers.

Maybe this is a second chance. I could start over and have a good life without the fear of saying or doing the wrong thing which always resulted in a beating. I could live freely. I could be free.

Sure, this would come with sacrifices like having no control over my bodily functions or having to get my food from a part of a human body that I'd rather not touch. In the end though, it will all be worth it. When I grow up maybe I'll have enough money to actually go to college and be who I want to be, no past to tear me down.

I can do this. I will do this because at the end of the day everyone has to make sacrifices if they want to reach that final goal and so for me, I guess having to grow up again will be my sacrifice. So, from now on im not going to fight these urges, instead I will give in no matter what the urge and maybe this wont be so bad after all.

CHAPTER 7

I SABELLA'S POV:

The man, who I have decided to continue call giant, was talking to the woman holding me while I ignored them and watched Luciano set the table not too far from where the giant, woman and I were gather next to the middle island in the kitchen. When he finished setting the table for, what I'm guessing is dinner; he looked up towards me and smiled, sending a small wave to me from where he stood.

Being unable to do anything I gargled disgustingly and huffed through my nose in return which made him laugh and made the woman and giant look down at me where I lay in the woman's arms.

After looking between Luciano and I, the giant lifted me from the woman's arms and laid me vertically in his arms so that I was facing him while he leaned against the island.

"And what's going on with you, my little bambina?" he cooed in a baby voice. {Baby}

I moved my arms up and down and kicked my legs as much as I could and a few odd sounds left my mouth, which made him smile down at me. My eyes widened when I realized that I couldn't stop myself and a moment later my diaper was filled. The tears poured from my eyes and a loud wail left my lips before I could stop it.

"Hey, hey shhh bambina, its okay shhh" the giant whispered as he pulled me to his chest. When his massive hand patted my diaper he realized what was wrong. He hummed in confusion, probably at the fact that he had changed me just a few minutes ago before we came downstairs.

He shrugged and made his way back upstairs without a word. I looked over his shoulder, still wailing and saw Luciano following us. We walked all the way to what I assume is now my room and I was laid down on the table, a mobile that played soft lullabies was put over my head in what I'm guessing is a failed attempt to calm down my cries.

Unaffected by my wails, the giant continued to change me, holding my squirming feet in the air to place a new clean diaper under me. He went as fast as he possibly could in hopes that I would calm down once it was all over.

Once it was over I was carefully brought back into the giants arms and rocked, his massive hand gently patting my back as he swayed from side to side. My cries slowly dwindled down to little sniffles and my lips turned to a pout while my eyes, which I'm sure were wide as ever were red from the crying, no doubt there were some lingering tears that didn't spill and made my eyes look wet.

"Shh there you go, you're alright," the giant whispered in my ear.

Seemingly out of nowhere, Luciano suddenly appeared in my line of vision. He made funny faces and gestures towards me in an attempt to make me laugh or, at the very least, smile before he announced that dinner was ready.

The giant picked up a small soft looking light pink blanket that was lying across the side of the crib. He gently covered me with it and held it in place with his hand on my back, his other hand resting under my bum so that I wouldn't slip from where I lay, my head on his shoulder.

I squirmed in his arms as he walked downstairs which made him chuckle until we both heard a crash coming from a room downstairs. The giant carefully moved me from his shoulder to rest in the crook of his elbow, probably to make sure I hadn't fallen asleep before yelling out "Gemma? Are you okay? What happened?"

"I'm fine Leonzio, Max dropped the forks" Gemma shouted back.

Huh. So the woman's name is Gemma and the giants name is Leonzio. Nice. Gemma and Leo.

Because of the slight swaying Leo's arms made as he rushed downstairs the feeling of tiredness came over me, my lips parted wide and I lifted my arms in a way to stretch as I yawned, my hands clenched into fists and my eyes closed tightly. Unfortunately, the sounds of heavy footsteps and yelling left me unable to sleep despite the rocking motion from his arms as he continued down the stairs.

I began to whine but something was quickly place in my mouth and I automatically began to suck on it, creating clicking noises. It didn't last long though, once we reached the kitchen I was carefully placed into Gemma's arms and the object was removed from my mouth only to, moments later be replaced with her nipple.

Knowing what was about to happen I sucked up what little pride I hoped I had left and began to nurse on the nipple with the knowledge that this was going to be the only way I will be eating for a while.

My hand came up to grip the top of her shirt that she had pulled up while I ate so that I could distract myself from the embarrassing moment and I noticed in the corner of my eye that Leo was standing behind Gemma's chair just watching us with a smile on his face. But soon, as if coming out of a trance he shook his head and realized that his sons were in the room and doing whatever they could to not look over at us so he took the blanket that he brought from the crib upstairs and placed it over Gemma's shoulder, covering both me and anything inappropriate for the boys.

I heard many sighs of relief shortly after but I paid no mind to it as I ate. It was not too much later that I was full and whined at the uncomfortable feeling bubbling up inside me. I was pulled up into Leo's arms again and was laid on his towel-covered shoulder while he patted my back and swayed slightly from side to side.

The more he patted my back the higher the ball of pressure moved up my throat until I vomited down his back. Thankfully he thought ahead and put the towel over his shoulder so that he didn't get any of the vomit on him. However, the burning in my throat seemed to be worse than when I was normal and caused another round of tears and wails to escape through my lips.

Leo shushed me and rocked back and forth, continuing to pat my back lightly to ensure that I had nothing else waiting to come out before he wiped my mouth, handed me to Gemma and put the towel into what I assume is the laundry room.

My eyes started to get heavy with sleep as I lay in Gemma's arms and before I know it, I'm placed in a carrier. I begin to whine as I'm placed in a new position but someone rocking the carrier and humming quickly stops it before it turns into wails. It doesn't take much longer after that for sleep to take over.

The next time I woke up it was dark and I couldn't see. There was music playing above me but being in a strange place in the dark made it sound slightly creepier than it meant to. I tried to turn my head in any direction to see if I could make out something familiar but I couldn't and a frustrated wail left my lips.

Suddenly the light flicked on and I was blinded for a moment but continued to cry, I just couldn't stop. I felt large hands wrap around me before I felt my body being dragged upwards, my head flopping back uncontrollably until the person fixed me in their arms. My cries began to dwindle as I settled in the strong arms and when they finally ceased I felt the vibration before I heard the laugh of the man holding me. Leonzio.

"You just wanted a cuddle, didn't you sweetheart?" he cooed as he rubbed my back.

He began to walk, leaving my room and turning down the dark hallway. I whimpered again in fear of the dark place but Leo just shushed me quietly and patted my back some more.

LEONZIO'S POV:

It's nearly midnight when I hear Isabella cry over the monitor. I groggily jump out of bed and rush to her side in fear she may be in some sort of danger. I chuckle when I realize that she only wanted to be held so I decided to move her to the master bedroom with Gemma and I. Since I had placed a small bassinet next to the bed for her earlier today it was rather convenient.

I notice that on the way to the room Isabella wines and squirms when we reach dark places so I make a mental note to pick up a night-light for her at some point during the day.

When I reach the room I see Gemma sitting up and her lamp on. She must have woken up from the monitor as well.

"Hey darling, go back to sleep. I got her." I whispered softly to her but she blinked away her sleep and shook her head with a small yawn.

"No its okay, its nearly time to feed her anyway so pass her here." She whispered back and held her arms out.

I carefully placed her into Gemma's arms before going around and climbing into my side of our bed. I lay next to my beautiful wife and watched as she fed our baby girl. I will never tire watching her, the look on her face as she gazes down at our daughter, caressing her cheek with her thumb as she eats.

I notice Belle's eyes start to droop and her mouth starts to slip from the nipple she was drinking from. Gemma signals me to take her to burp her before she falls asleep so I get up from the bed to grab the towel that was hanging on the bassinette and put it over my shoulder in case something other than gas comes out of her tiny mouth. After burping and swaddling her I walk around the room, slowly bouncing and swaying to make sure Belle is definitely asleep before placing her gently into the bassinette beside our bed and laying back down next to Gemma, pulling her to my chest so that we can go back to sleep.

CHAPTER 8

ISABELLA'S POV:

I wake up feeling cold. First as a soft breeze but then something much colder touches the backs of my now much more sensitive thighs. As I flutter my eyes open, getting use to the blinding sunlight coming from the window next to me, one of the first things I notice is that my legs are gently being held up in the air. The next thing I notice is a horrible indescribable smell and, judging by the grimace on Leo's face that is hovering over me, I'm pretty sure the smell was produced by me.

I start to whine, trying to gain back Leo's attention to continue changing as he has stopped to breathe in some fresh air from the open window beside us. The cold air and the freezing wet-wipe that is still pressed to my skin is becoming increasingly uncomfortable.

The smell doing little to calm me either as he still has yet to change the diaper that rests underneath me.

My body moves on its own accord and I wiggle around slightly but stop as I hear a distinct squishing sound before a deep groan from Leo who is now looking down at me in slight annoyance and amusement. We look each other in the eye. Neither of us really believing I had just done that but as the smell worsens we both know what has happened.

Just as I am about to burst into tears of both embarrassment and discomfort, Gemma glides into the room gracefully with a smile. She looks from me to Leo before bursting into a fit of giggles.

"I think this little one is ready for her first bath. Don't you think so, Leo?" she asks with a laugh.

"Seeing as she has managed to somehow spread this all over her back I don't really see another possible way to get this little monster clean again. I mean look at her, Gem! Its all over her back!" Leo replied with a chuckle.

Gemma leaves, stating that she is going to get everything ready whilst Leo tries to clean me as much as possible. When he's done he removes his shirt as to not get it dirty before laying me on his broad chest. With his long legs it doesn't take long for us to reach the master bedroom, and then their connected bathroom.

I watch through the mirror as Gemma turns her head and spots Leo standing in the doorway holding me to his chest. His large hand is big enough to cover and keep my whole body warm, as he didn't see the need to put another diaper on me or redress me.

After filling their sink, which was quite large and deep from my perspective, to about the half-way point, Gemma gestured for Leo to put me in before she bent down to get the baby body wash from one of the cupboards.

"So..." Leo began as he gently laid me down in the water, his large hands still supporting me as I got use to this new feeling. "I was thinking that maybe you would want to spend the day at the café and explain to everyone about you going on family leave. You can spend the time reorganizing the schedule and maybe hire a couple more people for while you're away?"

Gemma looked up at him in surprise, as if she hadn't yet thought about taking a leave. She stood up, going on her tiptoes as she smiled and kissed his lips. "Thank you for reminding me. I am going to have so much to do today." She laughed, shaking her head. "I can't believe I spaced on that!"

"That's what I'm here for, love." Leo smiled back.

They seemed to be lost in the moment, ruined, of course, by my lovely cries of fear as the level of the water started to freak me out.

I was definitely going to drown. The couple was quick to snap out of their loved up haze and looked to me in concern. Leo even pulled me right out of the sink and back into his chest, rocking slowly back and forth in an attempt to calm my frantic cries.

Once I was clam again they were quick to bathe me, seeing that they had wasted enough time already and they had to get ready to start the day. From my bassinette that they had laid me in once I was dressed, I watched their heads pass over me every so often, Leo stopping to run his finger along my cheek and Gemma stopping to kiss my forehead. I could hear their footsteps as they ran around, packing bags and cleaning the room.

"Babe I don't think I have enough milk to bottle. I can feed her now but I don't know what I'm going to do for the rest of the day." Gemma called out worriedly, but of course Leo was always one step ahead of her.

"Don't worry, I planned on taking her with me today and when I was buying all of her things I wasn't sure if you could breastfeed so I bought some formula as well, I can just give her that." He reassured her.

During my time here I have noticed that Leo's number one priority has always been Gemma, even before his own sons. He is extremely in-tuned with her emotions and always knows how to help her, no matter the situation. This is not the type of relationship that I have ever witnessed growing up, nor have I ever seen since leaving my so-called parents.

"Wow Leo! You've really thought of everything." Gemma exclaimed in surprise.

"Well I have to make sure my girls are happy, don't I?" Leo replied with a smile.

You could practically feel the love that sparked between the couple. It was like something out of a fairytale and it was beautiful. I was proud to be a part of this family, despite my current situation. I think that I am finally going to be happy, have a happy life with a good future and I am going to use it to my advantage and be the best possible person that I can be.

Leo's face suddenly came into view as he smiled at me and picked me up, kissing my head before laying me comfortably on his arm. His thumb stroked my cheek gently, feeling my pudgy soft cheek. He did this for a while, lost in the moment for, I have no idea how long as I had closed my eyes once I was settled in his arms. It was then that I got this sudden, intense feeling of confusion, like a fog took over my mind and I couldn't control my emotions or actions. A whine passed my lips and my eyes opened as I turned my head into Leo's chest, mouth in line with his nipple, as I got ready to eat. It seemed extremely logical at this moment that if Gemma was able to give my food from here, so would Leo.

Another whine left my mouth as there was something in the way of the nipple and I couldn't latch on. A moment, of what I'm sure was Leo's confusion, passed before his chest rumbled with a deep chuckle.

"No, no little one. Mummy is the one with the food my sweet girl." He said with a laugh as he turned towards Gemma who was already getting herself comfortable in the rocking chair next to the window. "You're a hungry little one aren't you?" he said again with a smile before he softly muttered, "My beautiful girl."

He carefully handed me over to Gemma who already had her shirt unbuttoned and her right breast out for me to quickly latch onto. I gulped down the milk like a starved child, not paying attention to the conversation they were having as I had I feeling that it might distract me from the wonderful milk that I was drinking. Even with feeling Leo kneeling down in front of us and him using his entire hand to cover my head while his thumb stroked my head, I tried really hard to not pay attention to how relaxing it was. Both their chests were pressed against me, rumbling as they talked. It felt so nice, like a lullaby and suddenly, before I could even stop it, I fell asleep.

LEONZIO'S POV:

My mind had been racing all night. How could this sweet girl have so little medical or family history? Are people truly that careless when it comes to innocent children?

I had today all planned out from the moment I looked at her file when we adopted her. I told Gemma to take today to change schedules and maybe hire a couple new people to help out while she's not there so she doesn't have to worry as much as I know she otherwise would have. This also clears up my day to get some things done that she doesn't know about, starting with a very promising hospital visit.

Currently, Bella's baby bags and her car seat have been placed in my car and now I'm just waiting for Gemma to finish saying goodbye to our sleeping baby girl and if this were a different situation I would hurry her up but, after having raising our three sons I know that this time between a mother and her child was something that shouldn't ever be rushed.

When she finally had her fill of our angle she handed her back to me before going out to her car. I followed her out and waved as she turned into the street before disappearing around the corner. Finally! I love my wife with every piece of my soul but I had work to do that she couldn't be near for.

I walked to my car and settled Bella into her car seat, double-checking she was strapped in tight. As I got into the drivers seat I connected my phone to the Bluetooth and called my right hand man, Marco.

"Morning Boss. What can I do for you?" He asked joyfully.

"I need you, my head of security and my head of the technical department to come and meet me at Sir. Johns Hospital (hopefully not a real hospital) as soon as possible. Tell them to bring any and all documents pertaining to protection technology because I know I asked them to start working on some new ideas together some time ago which means they should have plenty of things for me by now. Also, I need you to bring a few of our best bodyguards with you and my list of clients that I need to...have a chat with." I instructed.

"Got it Boss. I'll get everything together and I'll see you there. Would you like me to send the guards over before I go and get the department heads?"

"Yes. Tell them to actually meet me in front of my building they will come with me so send them down now, I'm a few minutes away."

"You got it Boss, I'll tell them now. Anything else?" he asked.

"No, just make sure that you and the others are there soon" I ordered and hung up.

I looked into the rearview mirror to take a peek at my sleeping angle while I waited for the light to change. She is so precious, so fragile. It's truly a wonder how she has survived even this long, being so pre-mature and not having the correct medical assessment. Its heartbreaking to know they just passed her over so quickly, not even giving her a second glace. What if she has a defect, or a serious illness that has already started to spread and become deadly? Until she is checked over by a doctor, the best one available, I will not stop worrying.

It wasn't much longer until I was parked in front of my office building and saw the two men, one brunette and one blonde, along with Marco waiting out front. I got out of the drivers seat and waved them over whilst opening the door to the back seat behind the drivers seat.

"Boss this is Zack," Marco introduced, pointing to the blonde man, "and this is David," he gestured towards the second man.

"Good morning Don Nicolosi" they greeted in unison.

"They are the best we have, sir" Marco informed me.

"Good, they will do. You may go now Marco, thank you and I'll be seeing you soon." I said in dismissal. "Now the two of you will be accompanying me to the hospital as we have delicate cargo that needs to be protected at all costs. You will follow behind me, you will be carrying equipment for me and under no circumstances are you to make your weapons visible to the public. This is a very important meeting and I do not need it fucked up by incompetent little boys who want to show people how tough they are. Is that understood?"

"Yes, Don Nicolosi."

"Get in the car, you guys are up front driving." I instructed before slipping into the back seat, sliding into the middle seat to be closer to my 'precious cargo'.

I know they were both wondering what could be so special that they had to be so careful and I know that once they glanced behind them they both knew how serious the situation was and that if they failed in any way, shape or form they would essentially be signing their own death certificate. It was probably the first time in their lives that they paid attention to road rules and speeding signs, driving as carefully as possible all the way to the hospital. It was quite entertaining.

Once we arrived at the hospital David, who was in the passenger seat, came around to open my door, as I'm sure Marco had instructed him to do. Before stepping out of the car though I checked to see if Bella was still sleeping, which she thankfully was. I climbed out of the car and instructed one of the guards to collect Bella's bag and my briefcase whilst I got her out of her seat so that the other guard could detach her carrier from the base of the car seat and carry it for now.

The hospitals information desk was conveniently placed in the center of the ground floor and it was just my luck that there wasn't a line.

"Hello sir, how may I help you today?" the receptionist asked with a smile.

"I'm looking for the hospitals director. Where would their office be?"

"Do you have an appointment?"

"Yes" I lied.

"Her office is on the top floor, room 1164"

"Thank you ma'am" I said before heading for the elevators.

The ride up didn't take long nor was it difficult to find her room. I told the men to wait outside and guard the door before I stepped in, unannounced.

"Excuse me sir but you can't just barge in here like that. I am in the middle of a meeting and I'm going to have to ask you to leave. Now." The woman behind the desk instructed.

There was a man in the chair in front of her desk, and with just one look in my direction and I knew that he knew who I was. He shot up from his seat and grabbed a bunch of papers, starting to sweat as he stuttered out that they could continue their meeting another time. I smiled in reply to him and watched as he wormed his way around me and to the door. It shut with a loud slam that made Bella stir. I rocked her a bit and she, thankfully went back to sleep. I smiled down at her, proud that I could calm her so quickly.

"Well now you're free aren't you?" my voice dripping with sarcasm, which made her roll her eyes at me.

"What can I do for you today sir?" she asked.

"First, let me introduce myself. I am Leonzio Antonio Nicolosi."

"Pleasure to meet you Mr. Nicolosi, I am Dr. Debra Marlow. Now, what can I do for you?"

"I was told that this was the best hospital in the state. Am I correct?"

"Yes sir. We only employ the best doctors in each field and strive to have the best facilities and equipment available to both patients and doctors. Why do you ask?"

"Well I am looking to donate a large sum of money to your hospital, but only on the condition that when my family seeks medical attention they will only be treated by the best possible doctors and that we will be of top priority as well as having the best private room available."

"That's a lot to ask of Mr. Nicolosi. How much are you willing to donate?" she asked as she indicated for me to take a seat. She was interested now.

"Well lets start with you giving me a list of all equipment that needs replacing or upgrading, as well as costs for possible renovations, I want to know the cost of everything from x-ray machines to how much you pay for your plastic forks. While you are busy with that I am going to need you to assign the best pediatrician available to look over my daughter."

"Sir are you sure you have the money to pay for everything on this list? One piece of equipment on it's own could cost thousands of dollars. Are you prepared to pay that?"

"I think you're underestimating how rich I really am and that is something you should never do when someone if offering something like this. It's bad business. Do we have a deal, Dr. Marlow?" I asked as I stood up.

"Yes Mr. Nicolosi, we have a deal."

CHAPTER 9

LEONZIO'S POV:

Dr. Marlow agreed to my proposition and stood up to hold out her hand to shake on it before calling a doctor to come to her office. "Your doctor will be here soon." She informed me before starting to work on the list.

I turned and walked to the door inform the guards of the doctor that will be arriving shortly. Dr. Marlow worked fast, probably already having most annual payments on file as well as a list of the machinery she needed. It was shortly before there was a knock on the door that Dr. Marlow stood up and handed me the list. She gestured to the couch on the side of the room for us to sit as she let the pediatrician in.

While the door was open I shouted for Zach to bring my briefcase. Once I had handed Bella over to the doctor I laid the briefcase on the coffee table in front of the couch and placed the list on top of it. I turned to the doctor and glared, watching like a hawk that he wouldn't bring any harm to my little girl.

"Good morning sir, I am Dr. Dawson. What seems to be the issue with this little one?"

"She was three months premature, I don't have any of her family's medical history because she is adopted and her mother died during child birth and her father is unknown. The doctors at the hospital that she was born at didn't conduct any test on her, just cleaned her and handed her over to the orphanage. I was able to get some medical information about the mother but it was only that she was most likely doing drugs and possibly drinking heavily as well during the pregnancy. Aside from that, all I know right now to be a solid fact is her name, height, weight and that she is three days old." I informed him as I got her file out of my briefcase.

"That's not right. I'm going to book her in for a full body examination and I'm sure you like as much information on her as possible so I'll organize an allergy test for her as well. Depending on what the scans show we might have to keep her incubated for a while and on an IV drip to help with development. If there are organs that are undeveloped it may cause problems in the future so we will have to look out for all of that. I will also have a nurse with her at all times incase she starts to show signs of withdrawal from any drugs brought into her system by her mother."

"Thank you doctor." I nodded to him before turning to Dr. Marlow. "I'll take the list with me to a private room near where she is being tested and I'll be calling my lawyer and accountant to meet us there so that we can draw up a contract and get you that check."

"Of course Mr. Nicolosi, I'll show you where you can stay. Please follow me", she instructed as we all got up to head for the door.

On our way out I let David know to call my accountant and lawyer to meet us here so that we could get started on the paperwork while I wait for the doctor to finish Bella's check-up.

The room was in a quiet hallway close to the NICU, 3 floors down from Dr. Marlow's office. It had a bed and a table with a few chairs around it and a couch against the wall across from it. I set up my temporary workstation on the table and had Dr. Marlow sit across from me so that we could discuss what will be in the contract.

"I would like to inform you, Dr. Marlow, that I have very specific conditions when it comes to this agreement, all of which will be placed clearly in the contract that I expect you to sign in exchange for this donation. I expect full cooperation in this agreement which is part of the reason my lawyer is coming now to write out this contract.

If you feel at all uncomfortable I am allowing you to bring in a lawyer that represents the hospital, for your benefit."

"I understand Mr. Nicolosi, and thank you I will call one of the hospitals lawyers now. I'll be back in a minute." She said as she walked out the door.

I felt my phone vibrating in the pocket of my suit jacket and pick it up, answering without checking the caller ID.

"Nicolosi speaking. What do you want?"

"Boss its Marco, we're outside the hospital where are you?"

"8th floor near the NICU. I'll send David to meet you at the elevator." I reply before hanging up.

Opening my briefcase I dig through it to find the list of men and women that owe me money through a loan shark I work with. Each name had a file that was made up by my private investigator when their payment is overdue.

One name stuck out to me. He had quite a thick file, both from all the times he has loaned money from me and was late in paying it back and from all the dirt that my private investigator was able to uncover on him.

There were four pictures along with him own in the file, his own being a mug shot with his greasy hair and tank top that just horribly accentuates his potbelly. One of the photos was of his house, which looks more like a rundown shack, the second was of his wife who looks like the definition of depressed and if I looked any closer I could spot the telltale signs of abuse. The fading bruises and the mixture of fear and sadness in her eyes wouldn't usually be noticeable to anyone else unless you really looked.

The other two pictures were of his children, the older one a boy who looked to be about 10 years old and a girl who couldn't be more than 2 years old. The little girl looked happy, I'd put that down to childhood innocence. However, the picture of the young boy was taken on his way to school. He had his fists clenched in anger but his eyes looked sad. Other people around him were wearing shorts and t-shirts, which leads me to believe that it was a hot day when this was taken but he was wearing long jeans and a jumper.

The signs were all there and I struggled to hide my anger. This piece of pure scum was taking money from me to probably buy drugs and then going home to beat his wife and child. It was wrong and this is where my part in the arrangement comes in.

When cases like these come to me I make it my job to save the mistreated people in these types of families. For families like this one where the children come out with one parent with them I buy them a house, completely furnished and stocked with food when they get there and I set the parent up with a job to keep them stable. I will also pay for the children's school fees for two years so that they can save some extra money for themselves.

At the same time I get to have a new punching bag in the basement of my office building, which is always fun.

My focus was dragged away from those files to the door, which opened to reveal Dr. Marlow and Bella's doctor. I could see it on his face that there was bad news and he was trying to work out how best to tell me. My heart skipped a beat and my stomach flipped. I knew it was too good to be true. I finally get graced with this beautiful angle and she is going to be taken away from me just as quickly as I had gotten her.

"I'm sorry Mr. Nicolosi, but I have a few questions for you if that's okay" the doctor announced with a shaky voice.

"Of course. But first, how is my daughter?"

"Allergy wise she is healthy, meaning that she has none and we even tested her reactions to aesthetics as well as other general medications and found none which is great. Other than that she will need to be kept here in an incubator until she gets a bit stronger...." The doctor explained but trailed off at the end.

"What aren't you telling me? What is wrong with my daughter?" I asked him while I stood up. I was getting frustrated. I need to know how my little beauty is doing.

"That is where the questions come in. Mr. Nicolosi, has she ever had fit, like she would just cry and cry and nothing would calm her down?"

"The woman at the orphanage said that she had cried for about 2 hours straight and nothing calmed her. What has that got to do with my daughter's health?"

"Has she recently had any runny poo's or vomited after eating?"

"She had a really bad poo this morning and I think she vomited after eating yesterday, I think she just drank too fast."

"Any trouble breathing or jerking and twitching?"

"I think I noticed an irregular breath pattern once or twice. What is this about, doctor?"

"I'm sorry sir but now with your help we have confirmed that your daughter is unfortunately going through withdrawal. I am going to need you to contact your wife because, whilst she is not the child's birthmother she is her new mother figure and the best treatment that we can provide and that has proven to work best, especially in premature infants, is for the mother to come in and stay with the child in the NICU so that they can have as much skin-to-skin contact as possible. She will also need to breastfeed the child as it helps with the mother-child bonding and at the same time the milk provides essential nourishments, antibodies and other nutrients. Do you understand sir?"

I was speechless. My gaze dropped to my lap as I fell back into my chair. My emotions ranged from disbelief to sadness then anger and finally hope that she can get better. I nodded my head in reply to the doctor and he cleared his throat before continuing.

"In addition to the mother being with the child we will need....we will need to find out what drug was being used during the pregnancy and then..." the doctor took a deep breath, "and then put her back on those drugs." He finished and I saw him physically cringe back at the glare I gave him.

"You come in here to tell me that my 3 day old daughter is going through withdrawal and now you're telling me that you also want to put her back on it?! What the fuck is wrong with you?! Do you have a death wish? Huh?" I growled out to him, punching the desk in anger. "ANSWER ME!"

"I-I didn't mean it like that Mr. Nicolosi, I swear. We treat infants going through withdrawal the same was we treat adults going through withdrawal. We will give the child an average dose for her size and then wean her off. It would be dangerous to cut any child off cold turkey which means we need to take extra care with your daughter because she is not your average infant. Being three months premature has dangers in itself but if you add her current situation the dangers are tripled."

The doctor stood shaking in front of me. My glare was unwavering but I understood, doesn't mean that I have to like it though. Bella's birthmother had better be thankful she died because she wouldn't want me after her now. The reckless little bitch.

"How long will this weaning last? When can she come home?"

"Normally the weaning takes about eight weeks, sometimes longer, it depends on the child. However, as well as the weaning we also have to carefully monitor her general development so I would like to stay for a minimum of four months and we can see from there."

"Okay. When can I see my daughter?"

"I don't think it would be right for you to see her at the moment. Why don't you call your wife down here so that we can at least start her on one part of the treatment while we figure out what drug or drugs she was exposed to. I'll check if it is okay for you to see her once she gets here."

"Why can't I see her? What's happened?" I asked in panic.

"Watching a child go through withdrawal is an extremely distressing thing witness and at this stage of a child's withdrawal we recommend the parents don't visit the NICU. I'm sorry, Mr. Nicolosi."

How could this happen to such a little angle that hasn't even been on this earth for a full week? How can people be so reckless and cruel? I don't understand. The only thing I know that the moment is that the second that she is out of here she will be treated like a princess. That beautiful girl will receive nothing but the best and I will make sure she has the most amazing life anyone could dream of having.

I did answer the doctor for a moment, trying to gather my thoughts and digest all of this information. Finally, when I felt stable enough I asked him if there was anything else I should know about her health.

"Because of her current conditions we can't do any additional tests to look at the development of her organs which is a problem because some could have been damaged by the drugs and those that weren't could be underdeveloped and have potential to cause health problems in the future. We don't know much about that at the moment unfortunately but we can't do anything but wait until we get her stable." The doctor informed me in a regretful tone.

"Understood. I'll call me wife down now. Thank you doctor." I nodded to him before he turned and walked out the door.

A state of shock took over my body as I blankly stared at the door that the doctor had just walked out of. His words echoed painfully in my head and knowing that I couldn't see my little beauty because she was in such bad shape was eating away at my heart.

The faint reminder to call Gemma made my stomach drop. This news would break her heart. And what about the boys? They have grown so close to her in such little time, what are they going to do? I know that I will have to be strong, be the rock, the shoulder to cry on just as I have always been for them but this time, this time is going to be infinitely more difficult.

With the little courage that I still possessed in this moment I walked out of the room and down the hall to make the call but at the last second I realize I can't do it. I just stare at my phone in frustration. I have to do this in person because I know she is going to cry, she is going to need me now more than ever and I wouldn't be a good man, a good husband if I let her drive after hearing something like this.

After quite a bit of silent deliberation I call Luciano because I know that he is probably at home or out with friends.

"Hello?" he answers on the fourth ring.

"Luc, this is important. I don't care what you're doing I need you to do something for me as quickly as possible." I say with urgency.

"Yeah sure dad, what's happened?" he asks worriedly.

"I need you to go and get your mother from work, tell her its an emergency and I'm waiting for you at St. John's Hospital. On your way there I want you to pick up your brothers from school, I will call ahead and make sure that the school knows that they are leaving so there shouldn't be a problem. Do you understand?"

"Yeah dad I understand I'll ask one of my friends for a ride to her shop now. What's happened? Is it Bella? What's wrong with her?"

"Don't worry for now I just need you all to get here. Make sure you are the one driving, I don't like your mother driving when she's upset and I'll need you to keep the keys with you because I might send you and the boys back home, if not to stay there for the night then to at least bring a few bags of clothes and toiletries, okay?"

"Yeah. I'll see you soon, bye."

"Bye Luc, drive safe." I said and hung up.

I didn't waste a moment after hanging up with Luciano before calling up the boys school to tell them that there was a family emergency and that their mother and brother would be coming soon to get them. After some quick words of concern from the school's administration they agreed to let them out early and I hung up.

I took a deep breath to calm my racing heart andcollect my thoughts before I turned back down the hallway and stepped back intothe room, closing the door behind me. I need to get this contract written upand signed before they all get here and maybe organize a few extra beds so we can all stay the night.

CHAPTER 10

ISABELLA'S POV:

My chest felt heavy and I couldn't breathe properly. I tried to gasp for air and my eyes flew open and they suddenly connected with a man in a white coat like those evil people that made me this way. I didn't want them to take me or change me again. I was finally with a nice family who wanted nothing but the best in life for me. I couldn't go back.

I started to struggle, my body convulsing and the noises around me fading into the distance. I could hear my heart pounding in my ears but I could see everyone around me rushing to get things and I could tell that the man in the white coat was screaming at the other people around me.

My body continued to twitch and jerk around for a while until I suddenly became stiff. I couldn't move if I tried. Every few minutes my leg or arm would jerk out but other than that it was like I had become a statue. My breathing became a little better but it was still difficult to get air in but I at least I could breathe now.

More people started to crowd around me and despite my now completely stiff, unmoving form I had a major panic attack. I could faintly hear the annoying beeping noise speed up before I finally passed out.

When I woke up again I was able to turn my head from side to side and I noticed that there was only one woman there dressed in a nurse's uniform. I think my movement grabbed her attention because she turned to me and took in my form which had started to shiver which she had taken as me being cold. She left the room for a moment and came back not much later with a small blanket in her hand. It was only when she lifted something on top of me that I realized that I was in a glass case of some kind.

The nurse lifted the top of the case and picked me up out of it, being mindful of the needles and tubes connected to my body and gently placed me on a nearby table with a changing mat on it. She checked my diaper before swaddling me in the blanket and placing me back in the case then closed the top. She checked a few of the machines before walking out of the room again and leaving me alone.

A sudden wave of intense itchiness came over and I managed to move my head enough to rub my cheeks against the slightly rough blanket. I dug deep and rubbed my cheek hard against the fabric, not caring if it hurt, I just had to get rid of this feeling.

The parts of me that I was rubbing against the blankets soon became irritated and started to burn a little. Then, seemingly out of nowhere, all of the frustrations of not being able to get the itchiness away and my confusion of what was going on came out in one loud wail and once I got started I just couldn't seem to stop.

The door burst open and the man in the white coat rushed back in with a few nurses following behind him. My cries got louder and even though I was lifted into the arms of one of the nurses, all attempts in calming me down were futile.

I could hear faint snippets of the conversations going on around me over my cries but it was all so confusing, I didn't understand what was going on and all it did was make me cry even harder, to the point that I coughed and puked as I tried to get air in at the same time.

"Dr. Davis, I think you're going to need to go inform her father of her condition and get him to bring her mother in." one of the nurses said to the man in the white coat, the doctor.

"I know. I know." He sighed and walked towards me.

I could see him through my teary eyes as he brought his hand down and gently moved the blanket away from my face, probably to wipe the tears that were still falling. He sucked in a breath, my cries no longer being the most significant problem anymore as he unwrapped me completely from the blanket.

"She has burns. Who gave her the blanket?" he asked in shock without sparing the nurses a glance.

A burst of cold air hit where I had rubbed my skin on the blanket and what followed was an intense, indescribable pain. I screamed and screamed before continuing to cry. I couldn't hear or see anything around me anymore, all sounds drowned out by my cries and all sights washed away when my eyes squeezed shut from the pain.

I cried for what felt like eternity, the nurses doing everything they can to calm me down until I finally passed out again from exhaustion.

LEONZIO'S POV:

With a heavy sigh I moved my eyes towards Dr. Marlow who was now accompanied by her lawyer. As I opened my mouth to continue out negotiations a knock sounded at the door before it opened to reveal David and Marco who had, not only my heads of security and technical department but also my lawyer and accountant. It seems they waited downstairs so that they could all come up together.

Despite the fact that Dr. Marlow was present for my horrible news I had received about my daughter, and even though I'm not certain when her lawyer entered the room I'm sure she had heard some of it, they both acted as if the last five or ten minutes hadn't happened, which I am grateful for as it made it much easier for me to put on my normal cold stare as I greeted my men.

"Now that we are all here we can start. John I am going to need to here with your laptop so that you can write up our contract. I want this whole thing written up and signed as soon as possible. Is that understood?"

"Y-yes sir." John, my lawyer replied and speed walked to the table.

"Please, Dr. Marlow and-"

"Jane, Jane Wilde"

"Miss. Wilde. Please take a seat, both of you." I finished with, what I hope is a welcoming smile.

They both came to sit across from John and I. Adam, my accountant, looked at me, waiting for instructions so I pointed to the seat on the other side of me. He rushed to the seat and we all got started.

"I am agreeing to 'donate' enough money to help this hospital purchase new, better equipment and machines which will then go to help the patients in this hospital. In addition I agree to continue providing 'donations' like this when the hospital needs it. These donations will be coming out of my own pocket as it is in my interest to help the patients in this hospital, especially because my family could become regular residents. My plan is to make this hospital the best one, if not just in this state then in the country or even the world because I believe that my family only deserves the best and nothing less."

"Do you agree to this being in the contract Dr. Marlow?" John asks. Dr. Marlow looks at her lawyer who gives her a subtle nod so she knows she can verbally agree.

"Next, in addition to the 'donations' coming out of my own pocket I would like to build a private room for my family to stay in when we are here. I will allow you to use the room for other important people when it is not in use on the condition that I am asked first but my family and I will be of first priority when it comes to both the room and the doctors treating my family and I."

"I don't know if that is a possibility. The patient rooms are on the lower floors so they are closer to examination rooms, nurses and doctors. If you were to build a new room we'd have to remove another in exchange and we need all the rooms that we have already." Dr. Marlow explained.

"I am fully aware of that fact. However, the room that I am looking to build will be the size of one of your patient floors. It will have a nurse's station and I plan for it to be close to examination rooms and other units. It will need to be large and will be heavily secured. You will provide a list of doctors and nurses who will be looking after the patient and then each of them will be given an access card and will be required to have some form of identification on them to show to security before entering. The nurses on hand will be there for immediate assistance in case of emergency as well as possibly one or two doctors. My company will provide the security whenever the room is used. If it turns out that we add another floor to the hospital and move your offices up one level don't see where the problem lies."

"And these renovations will be funded by you, Mr. Nicolosi?" Jane asks.

"Yes and, in a show of appreciation I welcome you to design your offices however you like if we just simply add another level to your hospital."

"I think that when solid plans come out we can discuss this further but that offer is greatly appreciated. Although, if your main focus is security I don't think it is a smart move to have your 'room' in the hospital if the only thing needed to get onto the floor is a push of a button in an elevator." Jane expressed.

"The plan that I have for the elevators is quite simple really. Those access cards that the staff, including the security, will be given will also allow them access to the floor. There won't be a button for the floor; instead there will be a slot underneath the buttons where the card is scanned so that you can go to the floor. No-one besides those permitted to be on the floor will exit the elevator and I plan to control that by placing two security guards at the elevator doors with their own list of names with a photocopy of the persons identification and their reason for being on the floor. There will be two security guards per elevator as I noticed on my way in that there were three of them. The door to the stairs will also have two guards, each of them standing on one side of the door."

"So, basically, what you're saying is that whoever is staying, weather it be your family or someone or high importance, they'll be better protected than...well anyone ever" Dr. Marlow said with slight disbelief. I chuckled lightly and nodded. I will agree to you building on the hospital and using one of the floors here to turn into your own private one because I can see that attracting lots of important people and helps the hospitals reputation. I do have one condition though. I want to be included in the process and how the actual room that you will be sleeping in is set up in terms of medical equipment and furnisher, for example, the beds and bedside tables. There can be slight changes made if needed but overall on this request I will allow it as long as you agree to my conditions."

"Then we have a deal, Dr. Marlow," I said and stood to shake her hand. "Now, I would like to note that if anything in this contract is broken I will be stopping my 'donations' and anything done, renovation wise will be undone and you will have a lawsuit against you. Understood?"

"And if you are the one to break the contract, Mr. Nicolosi? What do we get?" Jane asked.

"If I were to breach the contract then we can set a certain amount of money that I will pay the hospital. Name your price."

"Sir, how much is everything on that list going to cost Mr. Nicolosi?" Jane asked Adam.

"About 3 maybe 4 million dollars miss." He replied.

"Then I feel its fair to double it and say that we want 8 million from you if you breach this contract."

"That's fair, Miss Wilde. Is that all there is?"

"Yes I think so. In short, we will be providing you with an entire floor to make your own with your own money and have the added benefit of being of top priority with that doctors who will be assigned your cases, in exchange for all of that you will involve me in the process of your renovations and you will be donating 4 million dollars to the hospital which will be used to purchase better medical equipment and machinery in an effort to make this hospital the best in the state." Dr. Marlow recounted.

"Great! And we have an understanding on what will happen if either of us breaches this contract?"

"Yes sir." Dr. Marlow said with a smile as she stood up and held her hand out for me to shake.

"Perfect. Do you have somewhere that John can print this out? Afterwards we can both read over it and sign it." I asked as I stood to shake her hand.

"Sure, I'll take you to my office right away but before that, is there anything else I can help with?"

"I am going to need some extra beds or a bigger room on this floor. My family and I will be staying overnight, possibly longer."

"I'll take care of that right away, Mr. Nicolosi." She said with a sympathetic smile before turning to John and telling him to follow her. Jane left with them and I sat back down to face my accountant once the door closed.

"I am going to need you to move 8 million into a separate account so that I can have the money ready if I need it. Also I want you to research how much this renovation is going to cost, include any extra expenses for typical hospital room furnisher that I can modify. For example, I plan to make some of the hospital beds queen or king sized, the length of the bed will also have to be taken into account because we are all very tall men in my family. The mattress and other furnisher will also be chosen by me but when researching just aim for expensive."

"Yes sir, anything else?"

"Maybe add in the expenses for the new offices as well. Furnisher and such."

"Of course." Adam replied and collected his things. I shook his hand in thanks and waved to the door as a cue for him to leave.

The door closed behind him and just as I was about to sit back down my phone rang and a picture of Gemma popped onto the screen. I breathed in deeply in an attempt to calm myself before I answered the phone.

"Gemma" I breathed out.

"Leo? Where are you? We're at the entrance of the hospital, what's happened? Are you okay?" she rushed out in panic.

"I'm fine. I'll come down and get you, just stay there"

"Okay but hurry. I love you." She muttered back.

"I love you too, Gem." I replied softly before hanging up.

I turned to Marco, David, Zack and the department heads and told them to go wait in another room but motioned for Marco to take my briefcase with him but leave all of Bella's things.

With a deep sigh I made my way out the door and got into the elevator to meet my family at the entrance of the hospital.

CHAPTER 11

GEMMA'S POV:

My nerves were through the roof and I could tell that my boys felt the same, their legs shaking up and down nervously and poor Luciano was going to pace a hole in the ground if he didn't calm down soon.

The wait for Leo to get here was torture. Every second dragged on and I was going out of my mind, not knowing who was hurt or what happened turning me into a teary, trembling wreck.

A whimper escaped my lips which caught Luciano's attention, he turned towards me and frowned. Seeing his mother cry must have shaken him a little because the next moment he was straightening his back and clearing his face of any worry in an effort to comfort me before he came over and pulled me into his chest. In any other situation I would have laughed at the fact that he could so easily and comfortably pull me into a hug like this, just like Leo would, because all my boys were already so tall, constantly towering over me and making me feel so tiny around them.

Luc hugged me tight and whispered comforting things in my ear as he stroked my back. It was all so overwhelming and I felt like I couldn't breathe. My arms circled around his waist and I held him just as tight as loud sobs escaped me.

It wasn't much until Leo came and gently pulled me away from Luc and into his arms. He shushed me and told me everything is going to be fine before leading the boys and I to the elevator. Through my teary eyes I was able to see him hit the button for 8th floor so I checked the list of departments that were on this floor and let out another sob as I saw the letters NICU.

I looked up to Leo in disbelief, trying to see if there was maybe some other reason that we were going to this floor but he shook his head at my silent question and I looked down to the ground, sobbing hysterically. I would have fallen to the ground if it weren't for Leo holding me up.

"No Leo. What's happened? Please you have to tell me! I just got her! I can't loose her now it's too soon! Leo please" I cried out as he pulled me to him.

"Sweetheart calm down. I'll explain everything once we get to the room okay? Everything will be okay and we can go see her soon. I promise." He whispered and kissed my head.

The elevator doors opened and we walked out with the boys trailing behind us. We got to the room and Leo slid the glass door open for us to walk in before telling us to have a seat at the table on the other side of the room. Once we were all settled he took a few deep breaths and sighed before joining us and grabbing my hand.

"First of all, I want you all to know that Bella is going to be okay. I brought her here this morning because I noticed that in her file they didn't provide any medical records which can be dangerous so after a few calls I realized that the doctor that delivered her didn't give her any of the usual tests. It was important to get these done as soon as possible and I didn't want to waste anymore time."

Leo paused for a moment and squeezed my hand for support before taking a deep, calming breath and continuing.

"The doctor came back to ask me some questions about her, possible symptoms. When I asked him if she was okay he told me that the allergy test that they preformed went well and she doesn't seem to be allergic to anything, which is great but when I asked if he knows anything else he said that they are having trouble seeing what parts of her are underdeveloped because it seems that she is going through..." he trailed off.

"What is it dad?" Luciano asked.

"She seems to be going through withdrawal but they aren't sure from what drugs yet." He finally admitted.

My heart broke. How could someone do this to such a sweet and innocent child? Their child? This can't be happening. Not to my little girl. No.

We all seemed to be in a state of shock. Not a single one of us uttering a word as we tried to process this new and horrifying information. We stayed like that, still as statues until Max broke the silence.

"I-I don't understand. What does that mean? How...?" he trailed off in a mixture of shock and confusion.

"It means that while Bella's birthmother was pregnant with her..." Leo began but stopped to take a deep breath as he clenched his other hand into a fist out of anger. "She was on drugs. The doctors aren't sure which one, or if there was just one drug that she was taking. Because everything that goes through the mother's body also goes through the baby's, Bella became addicted and when she was born she was suddenly cut off, cold turkey. It took a few days for the withdrawal to really kick in but apparently there were signs before that we had just put off as normal."

Once Leo finished explaining he went silent again, as did the rest of us as we tried to process all of this information.

"Can they help her?" Theo asked with a shaky voice.

"Yes. The treatment is the same that you would see for adults. First they would give her an average dose of the drug and from there they would less her intake until they were sure that she could safely come off it."

"Have they started yet? Can we see her?" Max asked hopefully.

"They haven't started yet because they still don't know what kind of drug it was and they can't take any blood yet because of her state. Being born as prematurely as she was has it's own risks but you add withdrawal to the equation and it becomes about 10 times more dangerous."

"So what? They're just leaving her to suffer until they find the right drug?" Luciano spat out as he shot up from his chair in anger. He looked like he wanted to punch something, make someone or something hurt as much as his defenseless baby sister is hurting.

"The is something that has been proven to work." Leo said and turned to face me and grabbed both of my hands in his. "Gem, you are going to need to stay with her. They call it 'Kangaroo Care'. You are going to need to be there with her, breastfeeding is a must because it will give her all the nutrients and such that she needs. You will also have to hold her; skin-to-skin contact is a must because it will help to build the mother-child bond. Do you understand Gem?"

"She needs me?" I asked with tears shining in my eyes.

"Yes, Tesoro, she needs you"

I can't stop the smile that comes onto my face. It's been so long since I have been needed in this way.

"I have to warn you though that seeing a child, any child, go through the stages of withdrawal is extremely difficult to witness. This is not going to be easy, okay?"

I nodded, unable to form coherent words at the moment. Leo mentioned that we had to wait for the doctor to come back and tell us that it was okay to see her so he motioned for me to get on the bed and relax until it was time to go.

LUCIANO'S POV:

I can't believe it! How could someone knowing put that beautiful, tiny little creature that had so peacefully fallen asleep in my arms just yesterday, in so much danger? I don't understand.

Anger consumed me and I was ready to kill someone and I'm sure dad is too but he has calmed himself for mum's sake. Theo and Max though, I can see it in their eyes, they are so angry, furious that this has happened but they also push their anger aside from mum's sake.

I lock eyes with dad and he points his head towards Theo and then the door before he whispers something in mum's eyes and gets up. I grab the sleeve of Theo's shirt and pull him up and drag him to the door with me. Once outside Theo doesn't waste a moment before kicking a nearby chair and throwing another one across the hall. I watch him calm down from his outburst for a moment before turning to dad who is now joined by Marco, his right hand man.

Marco opens dad's briefcase and pulls out a file which dad nods his head in approval to before taking it from Marco and handing it to me. I can feel Theo look at it over my shoulder as I open it. With just one quick skim over it we both look back up at dad in confusion.

"What is this?" Theo asks confused.

"It's a present that I think the three of us are going to need and make great use of in the coming months. That man," he said pointing to the picture of the fat greasy man, "has been beating his wife and child, gambling their money away and letting everyone but himself starve. The wife and children are going to be moved to a safe place and will have everything they need to start a new life. This piece of scum is going to have a new permanent home in my basement where I believe he will make an excellent punching bag. I was told the one at the gym was getting a bit worse for wear." Dad finished off with a smile.

I grinned back and looked down at the file again, this man was truly a piece of work and I will enjoy taking my anger, that has been aimed at a dead woman, out on him until my precious baby sister is healthy again.

Theo has now calmed down considerably which is great timing because the sound of footsteps coming down the hall lets us know that the doctor is on his way. I quickly hand the file back to dad to put in his briefcase before pushing Theo towards the door of the room that mum and Max were waiting in.

"Are you coming?" I ask dad on my way to the door.

"I'm just going to speak to the doctor first but ill be in soon, you go ahead." He said and I nodded in response.

When we got into the room I noticed that Max was sitting on the bed beside mum and she had freshened up a bit, there were no more dried tear tracks on her cheeks and the only way to tell that she had been crying was the fact that the tip of her nose was a bit red from constantly wiping and blowing it.

The room was quiet and the only thing you could hear was Max whispering things to mum in an attempt to cheer her up, not much worked but she cracked a small smile for his benefit.

A sudden bang interrupted the silence and we all turned to the door where a few moments later dad and the doctor walked in. Mum scrambled up from the bed and rushed to dad's side in front of the doctor.

"How is she? How's my little girl?" she asked with a shaky voice. She was trembling and dad wrapped his arm around her shoulders for support.

"She's doing better now and I think it's okay for you to see her for a bit. We have managed to take a blood sample so hopefully it won't be much longer until we figure out what drug she was addicted to." The doctor informed us. "Please follow me."

We walked together down the hall and through the doors of the NICU where we were suddenly hit with mixtures of cries, whines and giggles coming from babies all around us. There were so many and my heart hurt a little for the, not being in the world for long and already having to suffer and knowing that my baby sister was in here too only intensified that pain.

The doctor led us around the corner and through another door. The atmosphere in the room was tense, probably because this is where all the much sicker babies are kept, any number of them could die at any given moment. The cries in here somehow sounded worse, filled with a pain that no child should feel. My eyes watered at the sound but I quickly blinked the tears back before anyone could see.

We notice that the second half of the room is where the incubators are kept and there seems to be one with about 4 nurses standing around it unlike the others that had one, maybe two nurses standing by. The doctor seemed to quicken his pace towards it and I knew then that it was Bella in there. The nurses moved out of the way as we approached and once we could get a glimpse of her I heard mum gasp.

"What happened to her?" mum asked shocked.

"It's one of the symptoms, she gets an itchy feeling all over her body and then rubs any spot of open skin that she can on anything around her. Before that she had gotten cold and a nurse brought her a blanket, which she roughly rubbed herself against and caused these burns. We have put come cooling cream on the burns so they wont hurt her as much anymore and we had to sedate her once we took a blood sample so she wont be waking up for a while. Spend as much time as you like with her." The doctor told us before looking at her chart for a moment and walking away with two nurses.

Looking down at Bella all I could see was tubes and wires. She had that tube for oxygen in her nose and wires suck to her chest, she also was also connected to an IV drip and was only laying in a diaper, which looked too big for her tiny body. There were deep red burns on her chest, cheeks, legs and arms, her nose was red and her eyelashes were still wet, telling me that she had been crying before.

A nurse walked up to mum and asked her if she wanted to hold her. Mum looked at her in concern before asking if she was really allowed to which cause the nurse to give her a small, sympathetic smile in return before pressing some buttons and lifting the lid of the incubator. She gestured for mum to come around as she lifted Bella out and then handed her over.

Theo, Max and I watched silently as mum sat down in a nearby chair and dad walked over to the both of them. They started whispering to each other, dad placing a gentle hand on Bella's head. After talking to each other for another few minutes dad stood up and turned towards us, nodding his head down the hall to the door. Once the four of us were out of the NICU dad turned to us and spoke softly.

"I know you boys want to stay here and make sure everything is alright with Bella but I think you guys should head home for a bit, maybe get started on your homework and have dinner. You can come back later because I'll need you to bring some things for your mum and I as well as some dinner so she can feed Bella and if you want to stay here tonight I'm sure I can arrange something, but you guys should go cool off a bit. All of this is a lot to take in at once and I think you should just go home, relax and process."

Theo, Max and I nodded our heads in agreement after a moment of silence.

"Can we say goodbye to mum first?" Max asked.

"Sure" dad replied and turned to open the door.

The three of us slowly walked passed him and headed back to mum and Bella to say goodnight. We had each given mum a kiss on the cheek and Bella, a kiss on her little head before we turned away and made out way back to the room we were waiting in to get our things.

The drive home was tense and quiet as my brothers and I tried to process what had happened, how quickly our world started to crack. This little girl who we've only had for a day has already managed to worm her way into all of our heart and shatter them into millions of pieces.

By the time we got home none of us even wanted to look at each other so we all just went to our rooms and locked the doors. No words spoken until we had to go back to the hospital for dad.